I'm Reading About

The PILGRIMS

GALLOPADE

by Carole Marsh

Printed and Manufactured in Peachtree City, GA., USA www.gallopade.com

Book design: Susan Van Denhende

Editor: Janice Baker

Photo Credits: Cover and Page 30: Jean Leon Gerome Ferris, Library of Congress; Page 3: iclipart.com; Page 5: Architect of the Capitol; Page 7: NSpiers/Bigstock.com; Page 9: Robert Walter Weir, U.S. Capitol; Page 11: bv55/Bigstock.com; Page 13: Wikimedia Commons; Page 15A: HandmadePictures/Bigstock.com; 15B: bhofack22/Bigstock.com; 15C: SKopp, CC BY-SA 3.0; Page 17: User Musphot on Wikimedia Commons; Page 20: J. Andrews, Library of Congress; Page 22: Jean Leon Gerome Ferris, Library of Congress; Page 24: Swampyank at en.wikipedia, CC BY-SA 3.0; Page 26: Sutro Library, San Francisco, USA; Page 28A: patrimonio/Bigstock.com; 28B: Garland Armor Bricker, The Teaching of Agriculture in the High School, New York: Macmillan, 1911; Page 32A: Suchan/Bigstock.com; 32B: pdb1/Bigstock.com; Page 34A: Olexandr/Bigstock.com; 34B: The Igorot/Bigstock.com

The Pilgrims hold an important place in American history!

What is so special about the Pilgrims?

Let's read about them and see!

COLONIZATION

In the 1500s and 1600s, Spain, France, and England set up colonies in the New World. Why were colonies important?

- They provided new land to control.
- They provided resources like wood from trees.
- They provided new places for trade.

In short, colonies provided increased riches!

Colonies were also started by people looking for freedom of religion.

New Colonies

RELIGION

In England in the 1600s, everyone belonged
to the Church of England.
It was the law!

Some people did not want to belong to the
Church of England.
One such group became known as the "Pilgrims."

The Pilgrims wanted to separate from the church.
They wanted to worship in their own way.

English Cathedral

RELIGION

The Pilgrims wanted to start a new colony in America.
They got permission to settle
north of the Jamestown colony in Virginia.
In 1620, they set sail across the Atlantic Ocean!

The Pilgrims left their homes in order to:

- Separate from the Church of England
- Find religious freedom
- Start a new community based on their beliefs

Praying Before the Voyage

SHIPS

The Pilgrims started their journey with two ships. They were called the *Mayflower* and the *Speedwell.* Soon after leaving England, the *Speedwell* began to leak! Both ships had to return to dry land.

As many people as possible squeezed onto the *Mayflower.* The ship set sail again with 102 passengers and about 25–30 crew members. The Pilgrims were determined to get to America!

The *Mayflower* sailed for America on September 16, 1620.

The Mayflower

COLONISTS

Who were those brave colonists?
The group included men, women, and children.
The oldest person on board was 63 years old.
The youngest person was just one year old!

Only 40 of the 102 passengers were Pilgrims.
The others on the ship wanted to start a new life
in the New World, and maybe become rich!
The Pilgrims called them "the Strangers."

Pilgrim

SUPPLIES

The people on the *Mayflower* needed lots of supplies!
Fresh foods spoiled quickly,
so they took foods that would last, like:

Dried Beef
Bacon
Hard Biscuits
Oats
Dried Fruit
Cheese

Drinks included water, cider, and beer.

Food and Drink

STORAGE

Since the Pilgrims were starting a new life,
they needed lots of tools.

They needed household items like dishes and blankets.
They needed farming tools like shovels and spades.
They needed building tools like hammers and nails.
They needed weapons like guns and swords.

The Pilgrims had to neatly store everything
on the lower decks of the *Mayflower*!

Merchant Ship Like the Mayflower

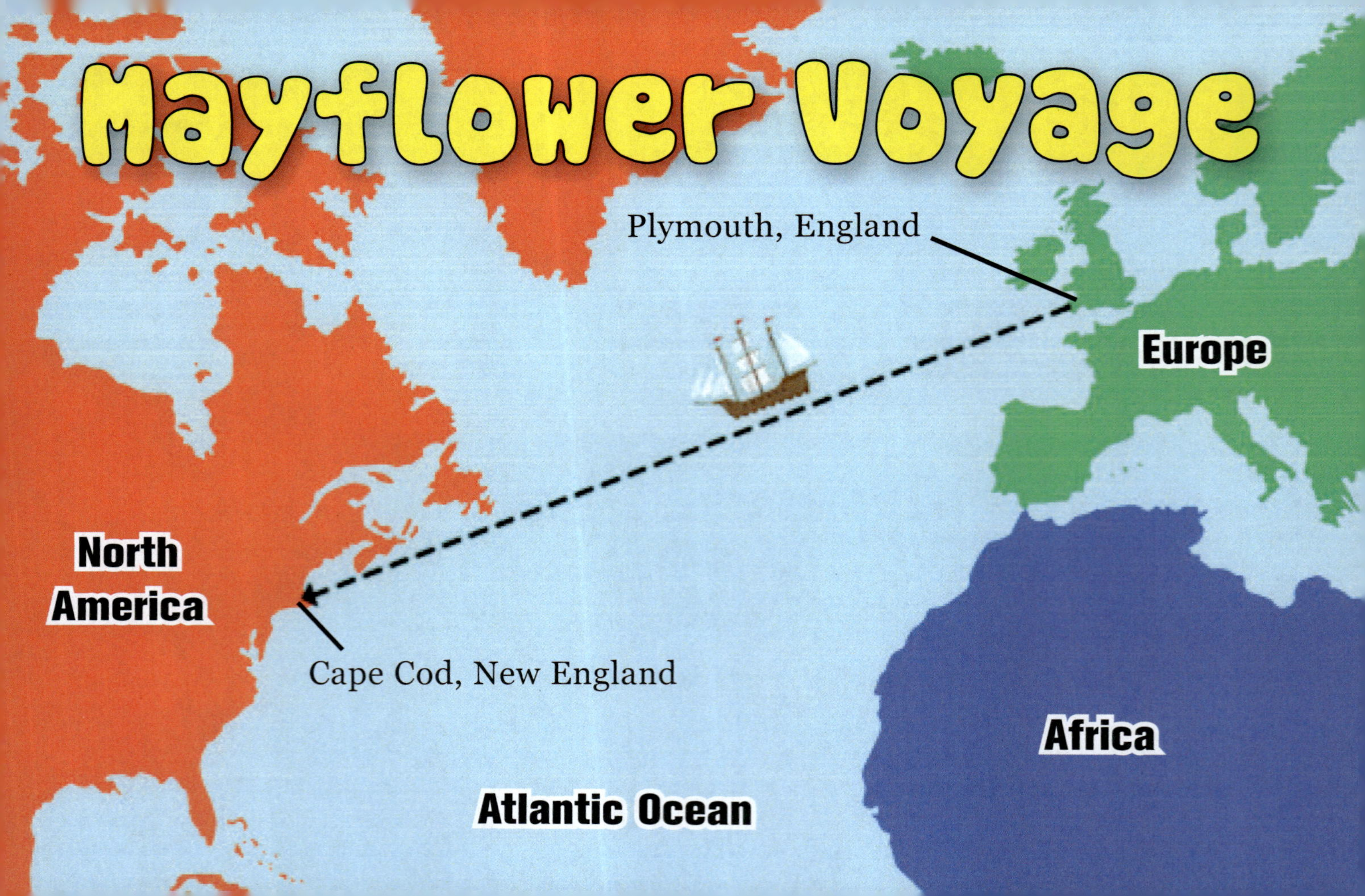
Mayflower Voyage
Plymouth, England
Europe
North America
Cape Cod, New England
Africa
Atlantic Ocean

The trip across the Atlantic Ocean took two months. It was a very rough trip for the passengers.

- The ship was very crowded.
- Rough seas made it hard to sleep.
- Big storms hit the ship.
- Many people became seasick.
- Many people got sick when the fresh food and fresh water ran out.

One sailor died during the journey, and one baby was born!

VOYAGE

Landing at Plymouth

LANDING

The *Mayflower* was supposed to land near what is now New York City. However, storms blew the ship off course. The *Mayflower* actually landed in present–day Massachusetts.

The Pilgrims searched the coastline for a good spot. They found a place with a good harbor, a river for fresh water, and flat land for crops. They named their settlement "Plymouth."

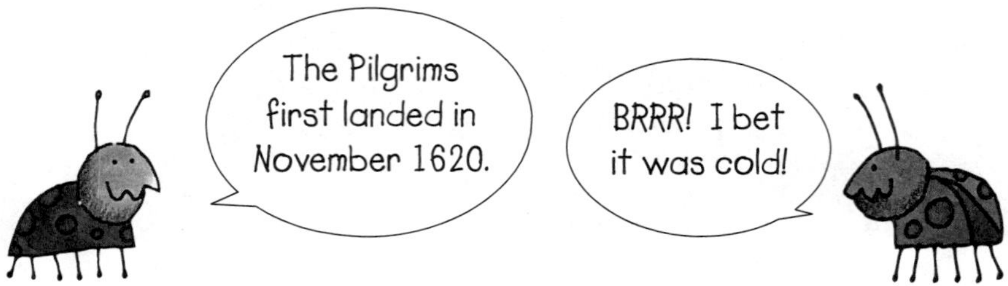

Mayflower Compact

When the *Mayflower* reached America, the colonists decided to make their own plan for government.

They drew up a special document called the "Mayflower Compact." It was an agreement that everyone would work hard and obey the laws of the colony. All the men signed the agreement.

The Mayflower Compact was the first written plan for government in America!

Colonial House

SETTLEMENT

The Pilgrims began to build their settlement in December 1620. The men built houses on land during the day and slept on the *Mayflower* at night.

Sadly, the winter was very difficult for the colonists. They did not have enough food, and it was too cold to plant crops. About half of the colonists died during the first winter.

Finally, by spring 1621, there were enough houses for the colonists to live in.

Samoset Speaks English

When spring arrived, the colonists met their neighbors.
A Wampanoag Indian named Samoset came to the colony.
He spoke English!
He had learned it from English sailors and fishermen.

A few days later, Samoset brought
another Indian named Squanto.
Squanto had lived in England and knew more English words.
Squanto introduced the colonists to his chief, Massasoit.
Plymouth's governor and Massasoit agreed to live in peace!

WAMPANOAG

Crops

Squanto helped the colonists in many ways:

- He taught them how to grow crops like corn, beans, and pumpkins.
- He taught them ways to hunt and fish for food.
- He helped them talk to the local Indians.

Without Squanto's help, the Plymouth Colony probably would not have survived!

Squanto taught the colonists to use dead fish to fertilize the soil.

First Thanksgiving

HARVEST

In the fall of 1621, the Plymouth Colony
had a good harvest!
The Pilgrims held a feast to thank God.
They invited the Wampanoag to join them.
For three days, the Pilgrims and Indians celebrated!

That event became known as the first Thanksgiving.
The foods they ate included:

Duck **Venison** **Fish** **Turkey** **Pumpkin** **Squash**

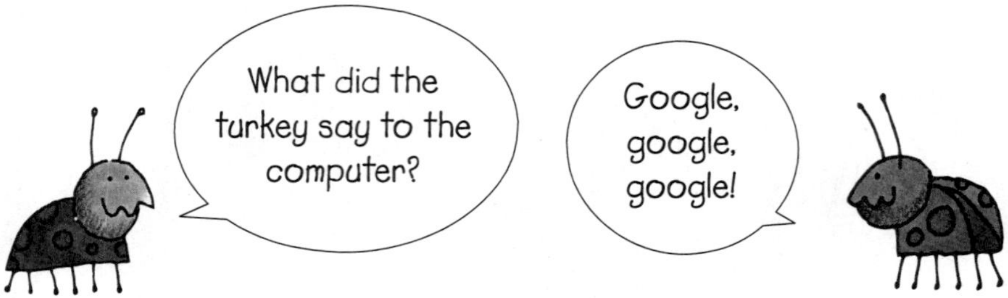

1620
Plymouth
Rock

Today, there is a famous rock in Plymouth Harbor
known as Plymouth Rock.
Some people say the Pilgrims first landed on that rock.
But no one knows for sure.

We do know that Plymouth Rock
is an important symbol in American history.
It helps us remember the brave men and women
who founded the Plymouth Colony.

Plymouth Rock is part of Pilgrim Memorial State Park.
You can see a replica of the *Mayflower* there, too!

Cool Colony

English Mastiff

Mayflower Replica

Governor William Bradford

DID YOU KNOW?

The Pilgrims founded the first colony in New England!
Read more fascinating facts about them:

- Two dogs—a spaniel and a mastiff—traveled on the *Mayflower.*
- Of the 102 colonists on the ship, about 30 were children.
- William Bradford was governor of the colony for over 30 years.
- The baby boy born on the *Mayflower* was named "Oceanus."

GLOSSARY

colony: a distant territory belonging to or under the control of a nation

compact: a formal agreement between two or more parties

harbor: a sheltered area near the coast where ships can be safe from storms

harvest: the gathering of a ripened crop

mastiff: a large, powerful type of dog often used as a guard dog

pilgrim: a person who makes a long journey for religious reasons

replica: an exact copy of something

venison: meat from a deer

GLOSSARY

architect: a person who designs buildings

expansion: the act of growing or becoming larger

expedition: a journey made by a group of people with a particular purpose

landmark: a building or place that was important in history

lightning rod: a metal rod placed high on a structure to redirect lightning harmlessly into the ground

memorial: something preserving the memory of a person or event

migrate: to move from a country or region to another

tram: a vehicle that runs on a track or on rails

LANDMARK

The Gateway Arch is a National Historic Landmark.

A National Historic Landmark is something very special to American history.
It can be a building, site, structure, or object.

Examples of other National Historic Landmarks are the Paul Revere House in Boston and the U.S. Capitol in Washington, D.C.

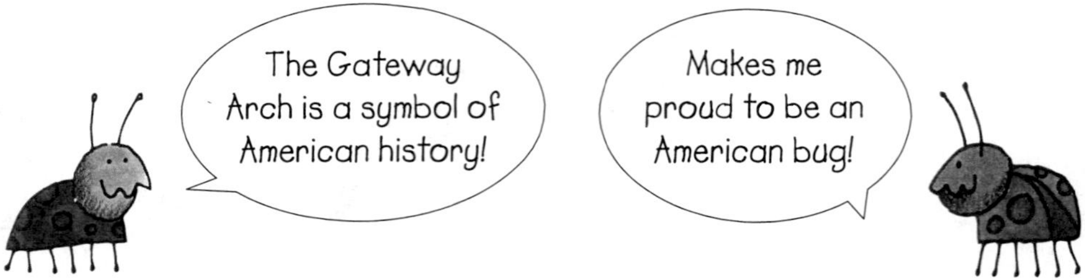